ONCE UPON A TIME IN THE MEADOW

A "Six Cousins" Story

by **ROSE SELAROSE**

A GOLDEN BOOK • NEW YORK
Western Publishing Company, Inc.
Racine, Wisconsin 53404

Originally published as
CHIARA E LE SUE AMICHE.
Copyright © 1981 by
Piero Dami Editore, Milan, Italy.

Once upon a time, six cousins lived by themselves in a cozy cottage in a meadow. Since there were no grownups there, the six little girls took care of each other.

One warm spring day, the cousins decided to have a picnic. Kate, who always pretended to be the mother, was tasting her special sauce.

"It's perfect!" she said to Betty, the smallest. "I'll just run out to pick some flowers for the table. Don't touch anything on the stove."

Kate arranged her bouquet on the table in the front yard.

"I wish Diana and Sara would come back with the strawberries," Betty said. "I can't wait to taste them."

"And where are Sally and Anne?" said Kate. "They left for the baker's hours ago. I do wish they'd hurry. Goodness knows what would happen to us without me to keep an eye on things!"

At last Anne and Sally came home with all kinds of treats from the bakery. And just as Kate started to fuss that the food would be cold and their picnic spoiled, Diana and Sara returned with their baskets full of sweet-smelling strawberries.

"I'll eat one small piece of chicken pie before I eat my dessert," said Betty.

"Yes, and you'll drink your milk, too," said Kate. She was only pretending to be cross.

Then what a lot of laughing and chattering there was. For the six cousins loved each other dearly.

And they had a wonderful picnic.

After lunch Anne suggested that
they play "dress up" in the attic.
Everyone thought that was a
splendid idea, even though Anne
would probably pick out the
prettiest costume for herself.

Kate had the keys to the attic so she went first.

"Watch out for Betty!" cried Diana—too late.

As usual Betty was in a hurry. She tripped and tumbled down the stairs. Luckily, she wasn't hurt.

It was cozy upstairs in the attic, and there were trunks filled with old clothes and toys. Each cousin soon found something to play with.

Sara looked at a dusty old book with pretty color pictures. Anne found a fan made of ostrich plumes and a lovely blue shawl. Kate found a long party dress, Betty a rag doll, and Sally a trumpet.

"I have a good idea," said Diana, holding up a black velvet coat. "Let's get dressed up and have a parade."

"Yes, yes!" they all cried, "a parade!"

The six cousins put on
their costumes and stood in
a row to admire each other.
"I'm the leader!" Sally
cried, and she began to
blow the trumpet. *Toot! Toot!*
Toot-a-toot-toot!

Down the stairs the little girls marched,
then out across the meadow. If they had not all
been laughing and singing, they might have heard

a soft sad whimpering when they neared
the edge of the woods. As it was, Sally stopped so
suddenly they almost piled on top of each other....

"What is it?" said Sara, who couldn't see over Sally's head.

There on the ground in the dark quiet woods was a rabbit caught in a hunter's trap.

"Oh, the poor thing," whispered Kate. "He must be in pain."

"We have to save him," said Diana.

Very carefully, so as not
to hurt him, the girls forced
open the trap.

Anne gently wrapped the
frightened animal in her
shawl.

Then they carried the
rabbit home.

He seemed to know that
the little girls were going to
help him. He didn't even try
to get away.

While Sara read instructions from the first-aid book, the other cousins set to work.

Diana brought scissors and a bottle of Kate's special medicine–honey and camomile tea.

Sally quickly heated some water to clean the rabbit's wounds.

Anne brought rolls
of bandages and fresh,
clean towels.

Then Betty gently
held the hurt leg while
Kate carefully wrapped it.

For the first few days
the rabbit hardly moved at
all. But as the weeks
passed, he grew much
stronger.

When he began to hop
about, Kate said it was
time to set him free.

That night the six cousins ran up to the attic to watch the rabbit leave. "His friends have come to meet him!" cried Betty.

"Good-by! Farewell!" called six happy cousins.